Spooky Scoops

'Spooky Scoops'
An original concept by Alison Donald
© Alison Donald

Illustrated by Mariia Kolker

Published by MAVERICK ARTS PUBLISHING LTD

Studio 11, City Business Centre, 6 Brighton Road,

Horsham, West Sussex, RH13 5BB

© Maverick Arts Publishing Limited November 2020

+44 (0)1403 256941

A CIP catalogue record for this book is available at the British Library.

ISBN 978-1-84886-730-7

www.maverickbooks.co.uk

Brown

This book is rated as: Brown Band (Guided Reading)

Spooky Scoops

Written by Alison Donald

Illustrated by Mariia Kolker

Chapter 1

If you looked at my street, you wouldn't see anything special about it. It's noisy, full of tall buildings, and there aren't enough trees. But for me, it's Sanaya heaven (I'm Sanaya by the way). Nothing ever changes on my street, which is perfect because I don't like change.

At the end of the road, there's a small ice cream shop. My best friend Jen and I have been going there since we were little. We have lots of great memories there—like the time my front tooth fell out or the time

Jen found a pound coin under the table. Every Friday, without fail, we go to the ice cream shop after school. We look forward to it all week long. Did I mention that Jen and I love ice cream? We *really* do.

But the year I turned nine, there was a particular Thursday when everything changed. It started like a typical Thursday. I woke up at 7:15 and had one piece of peanut butter toast cut diagonally. After school, I did my homework and watched my favourite show: 'Hashtag Screamers'. Everything was going to plan—just how I like it—until I took Chompers for his daily walk.

I clipped on his lead and he shot out the door, dragging me behind. He tugged and pulled me to the ice cream shop. Chompers cocked his head back and howled a long miserable howl.

The ice cream shop was boarded up. A notice on the door said, "Closed for Grand Re-opening Tomorrow – Under New Management". Did this mean that someone new had bought the shop and they were completely changing it? This was not okay!

My stomach felt icky. Our ice cream shop was just fine the way it was.

The next morning, when I got to school, there were already rumours flying around about the new owner of the ice cream shop. Some people had heard she was called Skeletina, and she never slept. Pretty odd stuff... who *was* this new owner?

That afternoon, Miss Bell, our teacher, was droning on about rivers. But Jen and I weren't really listening. We were thinking about the ice cream shop. A note landed beside my elbow. I slipped it inside my book and unfolded it:

I'm trying a new flavour today! Do you think they'll have Rocky Road? - Jen

I smiled and wrote back:

Maybe! Guess what I'm having: mint chocolate chip or mint chocolate chip? - Sanaya

Jen opened it and giggled. My message was funny

because it was true. I always order the same thing: two scoops of mint chocolate chip ice cream in a waffle cone. My order never changes. Did I mention that I don't like change?

So imagine how upset I was to find out that the new owner really *was* completely changing the ice cream shop! After school, we walked there to see it.

"Look," said Jen as she pointed at the sign.

"*Grand Opening: Spooky Scoops, a monster-themed ice cream shop,*" I read. The shop had been completely transformed. There were giant spiders and cobwebs in the windows. I also noticed a large sign that said 'no dogs allowed'.

"Cool. Let's check it out, Sanaya! It looks fun!" said Jen.

But I wasn't so sure. I had that icky feeling again.

"Oh c'mon Sanaya, our mums are already inside. Let's go," Jen insisted.

I swallowed hard. Something wasn't right. The hairs on the back of my neck stood up.

I felt like something bad was about to happen.

Chapter 2

"Hi girls," my mum said. Jen's mum, Mrs Ring, waved and smiled. They were having a coffee and chatting at a nearby table. Jen and I waved back, then turned to the counter to order our ice cream.

While Jen studied the ice cream, I had a look around. There were posters of monsters, ghouls, ghosts, and werewolves on the walls. A cat with no hair locked eyes with me. She was sleek and spooky. The name on her collar read 'Vanilla'.

I saw a statue of the ghoul from our favourite

show 'Hashtag Screamers'. I nudged Jen and pointed.

"Wow!" Jen cried. "This place is so cool."

I had to admit, Spooky Scoops *was* cool. Maybe I was overreacting. No one else looked scared.

"Hello girls, I'm Skeletina Sundae. How can I help you?" a pleasant voice came from behind the counter. She had three buns of wispy hair piled on top of her head that looked just like scoops of ice cream. Her face and hands looked pearly white and bony.

"Oh my gosh, you look like a real skeleton!" cried Jen.

"Why thank you," said Skeletina.

"It must take ages to do your make up each day," I said.

Skeletina chuckled. "It's taken me years to get this look just right. Now, which flavour would you like?"

Skeletina asked. "Our most popular flavours are: Cookies and Scream, Bloodberry Ripple, and Heavenly Ash."

"Bloodberry Ripple for me!" cried Jen.

"And I'll have two scoops of mint chocolate chip on a waffle cone please," I said.

"Sorry," replied Skeletina as she scooped and served Jen's Bloodberry Ripple. "We don't have that flavour, we only have spooky flavours."

Jen glanced sideways at me. She knew this wasn't going to go down well.

"How about Rocky Road To Death with a side of Slime?" Skeletina pointed to a shade of green ice cream. "It's minty and refreshing."

"No thanks," I said. I was trying to be cool but actually I was really annoyed. What kind of ice cream shop doesn't have mint chocolate chip?

We squeezed into a booth across from our mums.

"This tastes *amazing!*" said Jen. "Try some!" Her mum had a lick.

"Delicious," Mrs Ring said. "So good that I'll get my own cone!"

"I'll get one too!" said Mum and she followed Mrs Ring. "Sanaya? Are you sure you don't want a cone?"

"No thanks," I said and folded my arms. There was no way I was going to try any of the new flavours at Spooky Scoops. Ever.

Chapter 3

Over the next week, it seemed like I was the only one in the entire town who didn't want to try the ice cream at Spooky Scoops. Each day after school, there were long queues outside the ice cream parlour. Jen and our mums didn't just want to go to Spooky Scoops on Fridays, they wanted to go *every* day! Why was everyone suddenly eating so much ice cream?

"I have homework, Mum, please can we go home?" I asked on a Monday after school. I wanted to do my homework and watch 'Hashtag Screamers'.

Chompers whined, which meant he wanted to go home too. He didn't seem to like the look of all those dogs crowded round outside the shop.

"Sorry Sanaya, this won't take long. I just have such a strong craving," replied Mum.

I scratched my head. I really couldn't remember Mum loving ice cream *this* much.

Things at school were changing too. A lot of school work was about ice cream.

"Let's divide one litre of Cookies and Scream ice

cream between six people. How many millilitres will each person get?" Miss Bell asked.

We started learning about parts of the skeleton, spells, monsters and the history of vampires.

"Miss Bell," I said. "Aren't we supposed to be studying about rivers?"

But instead of answering my question, Miss Bell was scrolling through pictures of ice cream on her phone. Drool trickled down her chin. She looked different. Her face had become a bit... *furry*.

At lunchtime, Jen and I sat together as usual. I pulled out my cheese sandwich and she pulled out a flask and a spoon.

"What's that?" I asked.

"Ice cream," said Jen. She shovelled the spoon into her mouth. I looked all around me and other kids had brought flasks too.

"Jen, what is going on?! Why are you eating ice cream for lunch?" But Jen didn't look up. She shovelled the spoon faster and faster into her mouth.

"Jen!" I repeated.

When the ice cream was almost gone, Jen looked up. She had purple ice cream all around her mouth and she seemed to stare right through me.

She looked different. But I couldn't work out how until she smiled.

She had long, sharp, pointy... *fangs!*

"Jen, you have to stop eating so much ice cream."

"Ice cream," Jen repeated. "I love ice cream." It was like she couldn't hear me at all.

I ran home after school and flopped on my bed. Life was spinning out of control. Everything and everyone had changed. I needed things to go back to how they were.

It was time to investigate.

Chapter 4

On our next trip to Spooky Scoops, while Mum ordered her ice cream, I decided to slip away.

"I'll be right back, Mum," I said. "I just need the toilet."

But instead I tiptoed around the back of the counter, into the kitchen and hid. Skeletina soon whizzed in and jumped up to open a tall cupboard.

I heard loud clinking and clunking. She couldn't quite reach. She jumped again and again. CLINK, CLUNK.

Finally, she grabbed hold of a mug. She sped over to a kettle on the stove, where she accidentally spilled boiling water on her hands. My eyes widened. But Skeletina carried on as if nothing had happened, swiftly making a cup of tea and serving it to a customer.

I carefully got out of my hiding spot only to hear barking and howling. There were dogs outside pressed up against the kitchen window. They howled, just like Chompers did. Were the dogs after Vanilla, the hairless cat? What was going on?!

How did Skeletina not burn her hands? And what was that loud clattering sound when she was jumping up and down? Why were dogs howling outside the kitchen window?

Suddenly, it all made sense. The clinking and clunking were her bones and she didn't burn because she didn't have skin. The dogs were howling because they could smell bones!

Skeletina Sundae was a *real* skeleton!

I started making lists at home and at school. I split everyone into 'Normal Scoopers' and 'Super Scoopers'. Normal Scoopers were the people going into Spooky Scoops after school or work, like Mum. But Super Scoopers were the ones bringing flasks of ice cream to school, like Jen. I was most worried about the Super Scoopers—they were becoming more and more monstrous by the day. Some had

Super Scooper with fangs

Furry Super Scooper

soft fur growing on their face and hands, while some looked paler with sharper fangs. I drew sketches in my book. It was clear that the more ice cream that people ate, the more monstrous they became.

There must be something in the ice cream that was turning people into monsters.

I shivered. If that was true, I needed to work fast before I was the only human left in my town.

Chapter 5

"Jen, you're *not* going to believe this," I blurted out.

Jen looked up from her page. We were supposed to be writing book reports in the school library but Jen was doodling ice cream cones.

"I was in the kitchen at Spooky Scoops and..."

"Spooky Scoops!" Jen's face lit up. "I love Spooky Scoops. I love ice cream..." She had a glazed look in her eyes.

"Yes, well, anyways, I know for a *fact* that Skeletina Sundae is a *real* skeleton!" I carried on, but I could tell Jen was still thinking of ice cream. "And I'm certain that there is a secret ingredient in the ice cream that is slowly turning people into monsters."

Jen suddenly closed her book and stood up.

"Jen, please listen. We need to find out what is in this ice cream."

"I don't care," said Jen. "I love ice cream," she said again and walked off.

My heart sank. The old Jen would have listened. Maybe I needed proof.

Later, when I went to Spooky Scoops with my mum, I snuck back into the kitchen. This time, I had Mum's phone with me to collect evidence. I searched the countertops until I saw a shaker that said, 'Monster Flakes'. The fine print said, '*Sprinkle over any food and in no time, your normal human will be*

magnificently monstrous!'

So there *was* a secret ingredient! I took a picture
with Mum's phone.

Just then, I heard the quiet clickety-clack of
Skeletina's bones—she was coming! I quickly ducked
in the bottom cupboard and watched through a crack.

She pulled a tub of ice cream out of the freezer—
Bloodberry Ripple. She grabbed the shaker of 'Monster
Flakes' and gave it a few shakes. She then carried the
tub out to the shop and put it on the counter.

Now I knew for sure. I sneaked back to where my
mum, Jen and Mrs Ring were.

"Don't eat it!" I blurted.

"Don't be silly, Sanaya. Try some," said Mum.

"You'll love it," said Mrs Ring.

"It's the best," said Jen.

"Look what is in your ice cream," I said and I
showed them the picture I had taken.

But no one seemed to care. They all had a dreamy
look in their eyes.

"I've got to go," I said and bolted out the door.

It felt good to run. As I ran, the tears came. They

felt hot as they rolled down my cheeks. What was I going to do? No one would listen to me. I was so caught up in my own thoughts that I almost didn't hear someone calling my name.

"Sanaya! Stop! Sanaya!"

I stopped and turned around. It was a boy from my class called Haru.

"Sanaya, I need to talk to you," he said.

"Look, if it's about ice cream, I don't want to know. I'm sick of people talking about ice cream," I snapped.

"Ice cream?" he asked, puzzled. "No, I was coming over to see if you'd noticed that everyone around us is turning into monsters. Do you know what is going on? We seem to be the only normal-looking ones!"

Relief flooded through me. Finally, someone was on my side. "Yes, I've definitely noticed. I'm guessing you haven't had any ice cream from Spooky Spooks?"

"Nope," said Haru. "I can't eat ice cream. I'm allergic to milk. Why?"

I told him everything. About Skeletina's bones clacking, the secret ingredient and Jen and the other Super Scoopers.

"This is awful!" he cried.

My brain was churning trying to come up with a way to fix this. A huge truck lumbered past with a massive advert for cookies on the side.

"Cookies!" I said.

"What?" Haru looked confused.

"That's it! We can fix this! C'mon Haru, follow me."

Chapter 6

Back at my flat, I led Haru straight to the kitchen.

I frantically opened and closed cupboards. Mum would be back soon.

"Cookies, chocolate powder, sprinkles..." I listed as I grabbed whatever sweet, baking items I could find and shoved them in the blender.

"What are you doing?" asked Haru.

"It's simple. We're going to make our own sprinkles and swap them with the monster flakes."

Haru's eyes grew wide. He plugged in the blender and I knew he was on board.

Together, we sneaked around the back of the shop and slipped into the building. Haru pulled the fire alarm.

The noise was deafening. The customers all ran out the front door.

I bolted into the kitchen when I saw Skeletina coming. I hid in the cupboard again and watched as she checked for signs of fire. She looked puzzled and went out of the front door. I quickly dumped the monster flakes into the bin and put my homemade flakes in the shaker.

"Add this," a familiar voice said. I looked up just as Haru handed me a jar of cinnamon that he'd found on the side. I quickly added it to the shaker and screwed the lid on tight.

There was an angry hiss. Vanilla, the cat, slunk out from under a cupboard. Her narrow eyes watched us suspiciously and she started prowling towards us.

"Let's go," I whispered. We slipped out of the back

door. I could see my mum, Mrs Ring and Jen eating their ice cream in the distance but I didn't want them to see us.

The next day at school, Haru and I paid close attention to our teachers and classmates. At lunchtime, we compared our findings.

"I don't see a change yet." Haru's shoulders were slumped.

I sighed, "Me neither."

What if it was already too late?

Haru and I ate lunch together. It felt nice to be with someone normal. I glanced over at Jen. She had cast her spoon aside and was slurping ice cream straight from her flask. She didn't even notice I was gone.

The next day was the same.

"What if we were wrong?" I asked Haru. "What if things stay like this forever?"

But that afternoon, we noticed something. Miss Bell looked startled when she saw all the wall displays covered in monster drawings. "Let's put this work about skeletons away and pick up our textbooks," she said. "On page six, we will read about rivers."

Haru and I looked at each other and grinned. Miss Bell was snapping out of it!

Day by day, there were small changes.

"Let's skip Spooky Scoops today," said Mum. "I know you like to do your homework and watch 'Hashtag Screamers' after school."

I gave her a huge hug. "Thanks, Mum."

It took a while for Jen to get back to normal. After all, she was a Super Scooper and that meant she had eaten a massive amount of monster flakes.

"Can I sit with you guys?" she asked sheepishly one day. I nodded and then sighed with relief when she pulled out a tuna sandwich instead of a flask.

After school, we all walked home together. It was the first time in ages Jen and I had walked together and I couldn't stop smiling.

But suddenly we heard loud voices. Something wasn't right. Up ahead the mayor was trying to calm an angry mob of people outside Spooky Scoops.

Now that everyone was becoming human again, they looked scared and confused.

People wanted answers.

Chapter 7

Skeletina stood in the doorway clutching her cat, Vanilla, tightly to her chest. "The truth is..." she started, her voice cracking, "this isn't a costume. I'm a real skeleton."

CLOSED

The crowd gasped. I rolled my eyes. Finally! Now everyone knew the truth.

"Every time I open a new shop, the townspeople eventually figure out that I'm a skeleton and they chase me out of the town."

That must be horrible, I thought. But, like everyone else, I wanted to know more. I stepped closer to hear what she had to say.

"I thought that if I could change everyone else into monsters, vampires, ghouls, ghosts and werewolves, that you would accept me and I could still run my shop."

There were murmurs in the crowd. It was all starting to make a bit more sense.

"I like to think that as a town, we are quite accepting of different people and err... skeletons," said the mayor. "What you did was wrong, but perhaps we can give you another chance. After all, we do love your ice cream. But you must promise to never to change us into monsters again," he said.

"Thank you. I would love to stay! I'm so sorry." Skeletina looked down at her feet.

"I, for one, accept your apology," a man called out. "Your new ice cream is amazing!"

"Yes! Even better than before," agreed an old lady.

"I can't take credit for that," Skeletina replied. "I realised today that someone has replaced my secret ingredient with another one. That's what has made the ice cream really delicious! I only wish I knew the recipe!"

"Maybe we can help!" Haru said, stepping forward.

"We were the ones that found out about the monster flakes," I said, joining Haru. "We swapped it with our own creation. I am sure we could recreate it... on two conditions."

Chapter 8

After that day, nothing was the same. Things changed, but for the better. Now, after school I do my homework like before, but Jen and Haru come over and we watch 'Hashtag Screamers' together. Afterwards, we all walk Chompers. Chompers and the other dogs in the neighbourhood have settled down now. I think they finally got used to having a skeleton in the neighbourhood! And so have I. Jen and I still go for ice cream every Friday after school, but now Haru and his dad come too.

As for Skeletina, she's been trying really hard to make up for what she did. First of all, she bought some dairy-free ice cream just for Haru. And as for my second condition...

"Here it is, Sanaya, just what you asked for." Skeletina winked. She showed me a cone. It had two scoops of mint chocolate chip.

"Finally!" I beamed.

Skeletina continued to scoop. "I'm also adding one

scoop of Cookies and Scream, with sprinkles on top. It's a fantastic combination: the Sanaya Special!"

Skeletina handed me the ice cream. I examined it and I broke out in a sweat.

"Don't worry," Skeletina said. "The sprinkles are your very own recipe."

I got that icky feeling in my stomach. The feeling I get before I try something new. I took a deep breath and... I tried it!

I have to admit, it was delicious.

Discussion Points

1. What does Sanaya dislike the most?

2. What happened to the people who ate the ice cream from Spooky Scoops?

3. What was your favourite part of the story?

4. Who became a Super Scooper in the story?
a) Jen
b) Skeletina
c) Haru

5. Why do you think Skeletina pretended not to be a skeleton?

6. Who was your favourite character and why?

7. There were moments in the story when Sanaya had to face **change**. How did she deal with this?

8. What do you think happens after the end of the story?

Book Bands for Guided Reading

The Institute of Education book banding system is a scale of colours that reflects the various levels of reading difficulty. The bands are assigned by taking into account the content, the language style, the layout and phonics. Word, phrase and sentence level work is also taken into consideration.

The Maverick Readers Scheme is a bright, attractive range of books covering the pink to grey bands. All of these books have been book banded for guided reading to the industry standard and edited by a leading educational consultant.

To view the whole Maverick Readers scheme, visit our website at

www.maverickearlyreaders.com

Or scan the QR code to view our scheme instantly!

Pink
Red
Yellow
Blue
Green
Orange
Turquoise
Purple
Gold
White
Lime
Brown
Grey

Maverick Chapter Readers
(From Lime to Grey Band)